Daisy
the Hedgehog

written by **Tracey Thomson**

illustrated by **Ros Webb**

stories with children's wellbeing at heart

Daisy
the Hedgehog

Daisy the Hedgehog
is really quite sweet

She's gentle and caring
and lovely to meet

The trouble is no one
can see her kind heart

It's kept under prickles
that no one can part

So Daisy the Hedgehog
    spends time all alone

She doesn't have friends
    she can call on the phone

You see Daisy has prickles
Which look rather scary

This keeps friends away
    they are all a bit wary

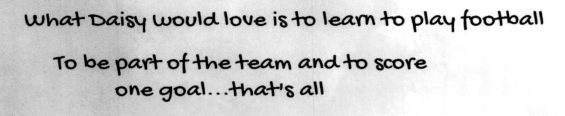

What Daisy would love is to learn to play football

To be part of the team and to score
one goal…that's all

But no one will let her join in with their game

She's not on the team because
she's not the same

They won't let her play
that's what she'd really like

But she might burst the ball
if it lands on her spikes!

One day as she sat all alone with her fears
There passed by a bird
who could see her sad tears

And so Mr Blackbird flew down from the sky
"Hello there young Daisy
What's wrong? Please don't cry!

You look really sad, but how bad can it be?
Would you like to talk over
your problem with me?"

"Oh no Mr Blackbird, you won't understand"
Said poor little Daisy waving her hand

"You can't make things better,
my problem's too tricky

The problem is ME!
I'm a hedgehog
who's prickly"

So day after day
    Daisy stays around home

  Without any friends
     ...she is always alone

She spends lots of time with
    her plants and her leaves

    And do you know?
Sometimes its magic she weaves!

With a small pinch of this
and a dash of the other

She knows how to make
lots of things from a flower

She mixes up lotions
and potions and such

It's hard to believe one so small
knows so much

Still, she'd rather play football
that's her hope and her dream

Oh, how great it would be
to be part of the team

How good it must feel
when you're scoring a goal

But each time she tries
she just makes a big hole

When her spikes touch the ball
it just bursts with a bang!

It feels so unfair she can't
play with the gang

Once again Mr Blackbird popped by for a visit
"Hello there young Daisy
Please tell me, what is it?

You look really sad, but how bad can it be?
Why won't you talk over
your problem with me?"

"Oh no, Mr Blackbird, you won't understand"
Said poor little Daisy, waving her hand

"You can't make
things better
my problem's too tricky

The problem is ME!
I'm a hedgehog
who's prickly"

Now wise Mr Blackbird
he knew from the start

That Daisy the Hedgehog
She had a kind heart

He flew to the meadow
Where down on the grass

A match has just started
Look, Mouse makes a pass

He kicks the ball hard
and he lands with a thud

Oh no, Mouse has hurt himself
Ouch! There is blood!

Mr Blackbird turned round
and he flew with great haste

"Come quickly young Daisy
there's no time to waste

Bring one of your potions
we need help from you

Little Mouse is in trouble
Quick - to the rescue!

Daisy ran onto the pitch
and she knew straight away

She had all the right skills
to make Mouse feel ok

With a dab of her cream
and a bandage on top

Mouse could
rejoin the game
with a skip
and a hop

Now everyone knows
   of young Daisy's rare talent

And no one is scared
   even though she is different

She still can't play football
   the ball would still burst

But she's part of the team
   She is now the team nurse

She cheers from the sidelines
and watches her mates

With her lotions and potions
nearby just in case

Printed in Great Britain
by Amazon